Baron
Rescue Dog

by Lola Schaefer

illustrated by Ned Butterfield

Richard C. Owen Publishers, Inc.
Katonah, New York

Baron is a German shepherd.
He is a rescue dog.
Today Baron is helping his master Ted
find a lost girl.

Baron uses his strong sense of smell
to track the girl.

He leads Ted up a mountain,
across a stream, through the woods,
and to a cave.

Baron crawls into the cave.

There's the girl.
She is shaking in the dark.

Baron grabs her sleeve
and gently pulls her out.

"Good dog, Baron!" says Ted.
"Good job!"

When the girl is safe with her family, Baron and Ted go home.

After some good food and sleep,
Baron and Ted are ready
for their next rescue call.

Baron and Ted are partners
and good friends.

They make a great rescue team!